Tornado
SUPERPOWER
Atomic breath
Magnetism
Fire ball
Crusher

For Naz, my great kaiju.

Published by Roaring Brook Press
Roaring Brook Press is a division of Holtzbrinck Publishing Holdings Limited Partnership
120 Broadway, New York, NY 10271 • mackids.com

Library of Congress Control Number: 2021906556
ISBN 978-1-250-77612-9

Our books may be purchased in bulk for promotional, educational, or business use.
Please contact your local bookseller or the Macmillan Corporate and Premium Sales Department
at (800) 221-7945 ext. 5442 or by email at MacmillanSpecialMarkets@macmillan.com.

First edition, 2022 • Book design by Aram Kim
The illustrations in this book were created with watercolor and ink and compiled digitally.
Printed in China by Hung Hing Off-set Printing Co. Ltd., Heshan City, Guangdong Province

1 3 5 7 9 10 8 6 4 2

ANZU
THE GREAT
KAIJU
Benson Shum
Roaring Brook Press
New York

All great kaiju are born with a superpower to strike fear in the heart of their given city.

Anzu wanted to be a great kaiju and make his family proud.
But he had one problem.

Anzu was born with the power of . . .

. . . flowers.

Anzu wasn't what you would call *terrifying*,

One day, Anzu came of age. And like all kaiju before him, he received his city.
ANZU
HAPPY KAIJU DAY

Anzu could not wait to cause mayhem.
Hi-ya!

But Mom and Dad thought some hands-on
lessons would be helpful first.

SHAZAM!

"A great kaiju summons storms to terrorize their city," Mom said.

"Make it rain?" asked Anzu. "I'll try."
He reached for the sky and . . .

SWOOSH!

Garlands fluttered like strings of butterflies. Anzu's city danced the hula.

Hula!

"A great kaiju should bring destruction," Mom said. "Not dancing."

Anzu laid down his lei.

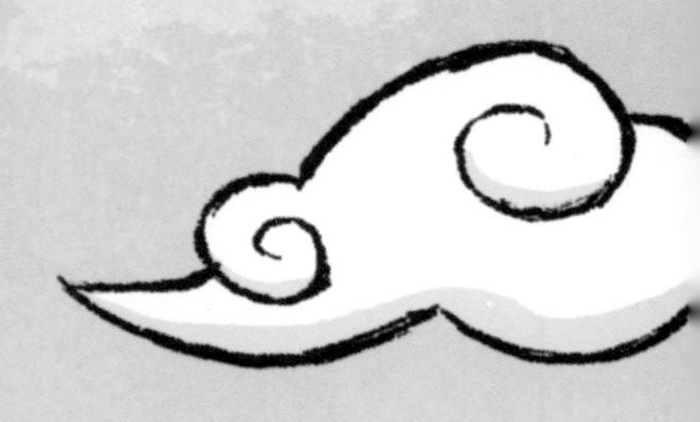

SMASH!

"A great kaiju hurls mountains to crush spirits," Dad said.

"Shake the earth?" Anzu asked. "I'll try."
He uprooted a tree and . . .

SHWACK!

Vines and flowers erupted, twirled, and swirled into a jungle of seesaws and slides.

See!

Saw!

"A great kaiju should unleash havoc," Dad said.
"NOT happiness."

Anzu STOMPED!
His city gathered seeds.
Anzu ROARED!
His city squealed
with delight.
More!
His city radiated with joy and laughter. Anzu's heart grew.

But his family's hopes crumbled.
Anzu wanted to wilt away.

"I'll never strike fear with my flower power."
"Am I even a kaiju?"

Thunderclouds rolled and rumbled. Grandma arose.

“Anzu, your ancestors are within you,” she said.
“You can do it. Awaken your belly. Ignite chaos.”

BOOM!
Anzu knew not to question Grandma.
So he drew in a deep breath and . . .

BOOO

OOM!

"I did it!" he roared.
His family held their heads high.
But when Anzu looked beneath the dirt and rubble,
he could not see his city's joy or hear their laughter.

His city lay silent, still, and solemn.
A great kaiju should feel powerful and strong, but Anzu felt empty.
Then an idea budded.

Anzu SWOOSHED!
Yay!

He SHWACKED.
Up!
Up!
Up!

He STOMPED.
Seeds!
Food!

And he ROARED.
Then Anzu drew in a deep breath and . . .

BLOOOooooomed.

Flowers flew, sprouted, and grew.
Anzu blossomed with pride.

The city worshipped their kaiju with cries of joy.
His family had never seen anything like it.

They realized Anzu did strike at the heart of his city–
but in his own way.

"I may not strike fear like a great kaiju," said Anzu. "But I am a good kaiju."

"Anzu," his family said.

"You are not a good kaiju . . .
You are an *extraordinary* kaiju,
and we are so proud of you."

SUPERPOWER
Strong